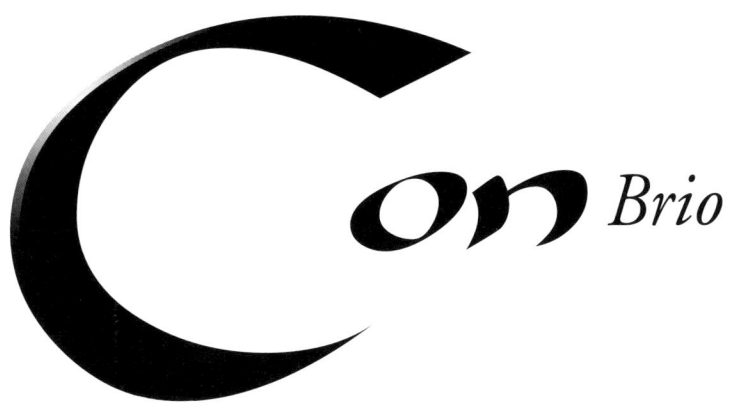

Con Brio

A Pictorial Essay of the Sydney Conservatorium of Music

Photographs by **Claude L.T. Ho**
Text by **Meldi Arkinstall**

Sydney Conservatorium of Music Foundation

Contents

Foreword

In 2001 when musicians returned to the wonderful "new" building in Macquarie Street from their temporary residence in the Australian Technology Park, the Sydney Conservatorium of Music once again became one of the most important cultural icons in our city.

For some years the historic premises had been swathed in scaffolding and industrial plastic. No one really knew what to expect. The unveiling proved the architect's vision to be a triumph. And then everyone wanted to "see" it.

At that time Elaine Chia was the Development Officer of the Con and she asked the Foundation if we could organize guided tours similar to those in museums. A volunteer group was established and to this day these dedicated and enthusiastic people proudly conduct tours ~ indeed they're booked out for months in advance!

One of the volunteers was a quiet, gentle man ~ we didn't know much about him ~ but he was always there, just when we needed him. One day Elaine asked if I realized that Claude (Ho) was an internationally acclaimed photographer.

He'd mentioned to her that it was sad that photographs of the new buildings depicted the architecture but no musicians, no people! Perhaps, he said, we might allow him to take some photographs of the "living con" and publish them in a book?

Claude began his mission. Soon he seemed to know every student and teacher by name and he became a much-loved sight in the corridors and halls. Foundation meetings became exciting photography exhibitions as we poured over dozens of shots from the latest rehearsals and performances. Each of the photographs made us smile ~ they were fully of happy musicians ~ sons, daughters, friends of ours. The project of editing them down to a suitable number for the book was daunting.

And then of course we needed some text. Who could we find to write the accompaniment to Claude's beautiful images?

Meldi Arkinstall could not have fulfilled our criteria better. Meldi had studied flute at the Con and after a career as a practicing musician, had decided to become a journalist. Although she had help from many people, it was her own connections from her days at the Con that opened a lot of the doors.

So slowly, over a period of months, the envelopes of photographs were sorted and the "shape" of the book emerged ~ a truly beautiful pictorial essay about music-making in Macquarie Street.

Thank you Claude and Meldi and all the members of the "team" who have brought it to fruition.

The Foundation of the Sydney Conservatorium of Music is very proud to bring you this celebration of the living Con.

Nola Charles
Chairman, Sydney Conservatorium of Music Foundation
August 2004

The Conservatorium's Concert Coordinator Steven Burns with volunteer Wilhelmena van Dorp

Volunteers Ray Newell and Yvonne Spielman on front desk duty

Acknowledgements

First published in 2004

Copyright© Sydney Conservatorium of
Music Foundation

All rights reserved. No parts of this book
may be reproduced or transmitted in any form
or by any means without prior permission
in writing from the publisher.

Publisher: Sydney Conservatorium of
Music Foundation
Macquarie Street, Sydney 2000
NSW, Australia.

Tel: 02-9351 1342

ISBN: 0-646-43897-2

Designed by: Joe Tsang
Edited by: Bridget Elliot

Printed in Hong Kong SAR

4

I express my gratitude and appreciation to the following people who have
been involved in various ways in the making of this book: Conservatorium
staff members Steven Burns, Paige Shipway and Sanchia Osborne, who gave
me their full and patient support, and lecturers Gerard Willems and Nicole
Dorigo for their encouragement and guidance.

Elaine Chia, a former staff member, helped to initiate this project and gave me
much support. I also thank Bligh Glass of the Conservatorium Library who
made the historical photographs available to this project.

I thank all the staff members for their patience to me during their teaching or
rehearsal sessions. These include Susanne James and her colleagues at the
Conservatorium Music Access Centre, as well as principal Barbara McCrae
and teacher Alan Scots-Roger of the Conservatorium High School.

Last but by no means least, I thank the Chairman of the Sydney
Conservatorium of Music Foundation, Nola Charles, and Foundation
members Ray Newell, Liz Loxton and Jane Rowden for their unceasing co-
operation over an extended period.

Claude L.T. Ho

Peter McCallum recommended me to the Sydney Conservatorium of Music
Foundation for this project, for which I am most appreciative. It has been a
wonderful task and a fulfilling means of combining my love for music with
my career in journalism.

During my research I have been helped by more Conservatorium people past
and present than it is possible to thank here. Among them though, I am
especially grateful to three former directors ~ John Painter, Ronald Smart and
John Hopkins. I also thank the Chairman of the Conservatorium Foundation,
Nola Charles, for her passion and inspiration, and Foundation members Ray
Newell, for his interviews, and Jane Rowden and Liz Loxton for their
assistance. Bligh Glass generously gave of her time in the Conservatorium
Library, while Dianne Collins' book, *Sounds from the Stables*, was an invalu-
able reference.

Finally I thank Bridget Elliot and Gavin Souter for their editorial suggestions.

Meldi Arkinstall

Re-prints of photographs from pages
7,8,9,10 (below), 13 (top), 69 (below)
courtesy of the Conservatorium Library.

Prelude

I would like to think that the 120 or so photographs in this book are all related to "the living Con". It is my wish therefore that this book be regarded as a testimony to the lecturers, staff and to every student who ever has set foot in this musical icon. I salute them all!

The project has evoked happy memories of the early 1960s when I undertook private clarinet tuition at the Con. Having recently returned to Australia to retire after a career as a professional photographer that spanned 37 years and included work in over 20 countries, it was with great pleasure that I accepted the Sydney Conservatorium of Music Foundation's offer to undertake this project. There is a sense for me of having come full circle, and what better assignment could there be for a music lover?

I find that creating a photographic image of an individual is a very special process that is perhaps akin to writing a poem.

I am therefore very honoured to have been given the opportunity to convey the intrinsic poetry of The Con - its architecture, its ambience and the many talented individuals within its walls - with my camera.

Claude L.T. Ho

Walk into the Sydney Conservatorium of Music and you enter a creative powerhouse in which intellect and inspiration combine. Music emanates from every corner of the building ~ an energetic soprano practising her scales merges with the sound of a trombonist warming up. This book aims to celebrate the many talented musicians and administrators who have made the "Con" the vibrant centre of excellence that it is today.

These people are no less extraordinary than their environment and the Con's restored building is very much part of this celebration. When it re-opened in August 2001 *The Sydney Morning Herald* declared of the new building: "It puts students in the streets, music in the air, light in the earth, energy in the Greenway and archaeology in an enchanted public space... music is everywhere."

The Con has gone through many stages in its history and holds a few surprises. Few people know that rifles were stored behind its walls during World War I or that one of its directors, Eugene Goosens, conducted the British premier of Stravinsky's *The Rite of Spring*.

Con Brio is not a history of the Conservatorium, however. Rather, it is a kaleidoscopic perspective ~ a selection of images vividly captured by photographer Claude L.T. Ho, combined with interviews, recollections and personal anecdotes that serve to reflect the many musical activities and the diverse personalities there.

Meldi Arkinstall

The Student Orchestra c.1916 (above) and student Carolyn Chan
performing in the Verbrugghen Hall (opposite)

The Making of History

The building that houses the Conservatorium was completed in 1821
to accommodate the horses and servants of the Governor. Modelled
on two castles in Scotland, the stables were situated down the road
from the Governor's residence, which was built in 1847.

What is now the Verbrugghen Hall was then an open quadrangle in
which horses used to exercise. Although suggestions to turn the
stables into a home for the city's musicians were not taken seriously
at first, it became obvious that the stables' prime location and the
relatively low cost involved in their conversion made them a viable
option.

So it was that the building was gutted and the central yard became
a concert hall; the interior was painted white and green and the
entrance was moved from the southern wall to the western wall facing
Macquarie Street.

By 1914 musicians were using the building and the Conservatorium
had adopted a Constitution and a Council. Applications for the
position of director of the Conservatorium were circulated
throughout Australasia, Britain, Europe, Canada and the United
States. The advertisement included a salary of 1250 pounds and
attracted 173 applications.

The Conservatorium opened officially in 1915 and although he did
not stand out in the first round of applications, Henri Verbrugghen
was eventually successful.

Henri Verbrugghen 1915-1921

A Belgian violinist, Verbrugghen was considered a prestigious
appointee because he was European. The Ensemble Unit's current
chair, David Miller, observes: "In Verbrugghen's day there was a
massive cultural cringe… The fact that Verbrugghen was a foreign
musician would have made him an important person in society."

Verbrugghen's appointment as director was announced to the press on May 20, 1915 and he sailed from Europe shortly thereafter. An article in the *Canon* newsletter in 1961, by Catherine Mackerras, described Verbrugghen as a man who "did not suffer fools gladly. He was a good judge of men; in four years I never once saw him lose his temper. It was he who first revealed to me the beauties of the Beethoven concerto; he introduced the great *Missa Solemnis* to Australia".

Summing up his significance to Sydney she wrote: "I think he was one who would have driven himself too hard wherever he was and we should count ourselves fortunate that he gave us what were probably the best six years of his life."

By 1916 the Conservatorium had 40 staff and 320 students and a year later the number of students had increased to 500. Teachers' salaries depended on student fees (and not government funding) so the only prerequisite for students was a desire to have lessons. Today students must undergo a rigorous audition process for study at the Conservatorium on any level. But the tension between funding and having enough students to fill the places is ever-present.

In early years the vocal and piano departments did not appoint heads of department because it was believed that no one in Australia was suitable. This inferiority complex still pervades the country's cultural life today, although fortunately to a much lesser extent.

The Conservatorium was not without its critics in those early years. Along with other private associations with a vested interest in teaching, the Musical Association of NSW tried to undermine the authority of the Conservatorium in the community. This attack may have been the result of a perceived lack of interest on the Conservatorium's part in gifted students, which could be interpreted as either "tall poppy syndrome" or uncertainty about what to do with these exceptional musicians once they had graduated. This is still an issue today to some degree.

With little or no operatic training available, the Conservatorium under Verbrugghen focused on chamber music. The level of govern-ment funding meant that an opera school was simply not possible.

Greenway Building prior to renovation in the early 1900s

Greenway Building under renovation c.1913

Having imported his string quartet from England, Verbrugghen insisted that it should be employed by the Conservatorium. He introduced the now famous Wednesday lunchtime concerts and made attendance compulsory for students. He set about educating not just students but the people of Sydney, holding concerts at schools and allowing the public to join orchestral and choral groups at the Conservatorium.

Verbrugghen admitted that he "loved England and the English. But I do not love their schools of music. Sydney's Conservatorium will be on the Continental system". This meant providing an all-round education. Verbrugghen regularly invited lecturers from the University of Sydney whose expertise covered a wide range of subjects including social evolution and history. He was renowned for his own comprehensive lecture-recitals that examined the works of the great composers.

In 1919 the state government allocated the Conservatorium Orchestra separate funding from the Conservatorium, making it the first state-funded orchestra in the English-speaking world. It would (much) later become the Sydney Symphony Orchestra. Constant touring kept the orchestra busy but Verbrugghen was not paid anything over and above his salary as director.

In 1921 Verbrugghen demanded a salary of 1500 pounds for each of the two roles, and pointed out to the government that he had conducted 450 concerts and 600 rehearsals in the previous three years. The government disagreed, and during a trip abroad Verbrugghen was offered a 25,000-dollar conductorship with the Minneapolis Symphony Orchestra. He accepted, to the dismay of Sydney's music community.

Dr Arundel Orchard 1923 – 1934

Under Verbrugghen the Australian Music Examinations Board (AMEB) was founded in 1918 and exams were held at the Conservatorium. Teaching had become formalised and the Conservatorium High School was set up in a single room.

Keyboard Laboratory, 2004

Composition class in the 1950s

After Verbrugghen's departure, however, the institution struggled and was threatened with closure. A lack of political support (including the withdrawal of state scholarships) did not help. The Conservatorium had to set about the daunting task of finding a replacement for Verbrugghen.

Melbourne-born Alfred Hill and Englishman Dr Arundel Orchard were the main contenders, and Dr Orchard was successful. Although not a brilliant musician, he founded several groups including the Sydney Madrigal and Chamber Music societies. Enjoying the company of the wealthy, Dr Orchard used his networking skills to obtain government approval for a tour of overseas conservatoriums in the late 1920s.

He started a Conservatorium Quartet to succeed the Verbrugghen Quartet, giving six concerts a year. The Conservatorium Orchestra had been disbanded by this time but Dr Orchard revitalised it and convinced the government to create permanent positions for some of the staff. Sixty student scholarships were provided by the government and the Con's fortunes started to improve.

Dr Orchard worked hard at wooing the press and private donors. He attracted famous artists including Nellie Melba, Jascha Heifetz (whom he convinced to donate 400 pounds for the purchase of orchestral scores) and Fritz Kreisler to the Conservatorium. He entertained their foibles, including Melba's preference for holding meetings with him in her car, rather than in the corridors of the Conservatorium.

In 1925 the Conservatorium Orchestra gave the first Australian performance of *The Planets* by Gustav Holst. It was so well received that the last movement had to be repeated. By 1929, however, the depression had struck. Despite the difficult times the Conservatorium Orchestra managed to give the "First Classical Music Broadcast Concert" from the Sydney Town Hall for the Australian Broadcasting Corporation (ABC).

Dr Orchard occupied himself with trying to introduce opera to the Conservatorium, with limited success. It was not to be until 1935 that Dr Edgar Bainton founded the Conservatorium Opera School with Roland Foster and Hilda Mulligan.

When he turned 65, Dr Orchard was forced to step down under retirement regulations introduced by the state government.

Edgar Bainton 1934 - 1948

Englishman Edgar Bainton was named as Dr Orchard's successor, despite widespread protest against employing a non-Australian. Critics pointed out that if Australians could serve as bishops in the Church, why not appoint a local as director of the Conservatorium?

Bainton had taken piano lessons with the student of a student of Clara Schumann and had previously been director of the Newcastle-on-Tyne Conservatorium for 20 years. He had conducted the first performance of *The Firebird* ballet suite by Stravinsky and under his directorship of the Conservatorium, renowned conductors including Malcolm Sargent, Thomas Beecham and Eugene Ormandy visited Australia to conduct the ABC's "Celebrity" concert series.

He had a passion for music education and was responsible for the introduction of music as a full subject for the high-school intermediate and leaving certificates.

Bainton was rightly proud of his role in establishing the Conservatorium's opera school in 1935. For the next 13 years it was the only place where the people of Sydney could enjoy opera. By 1938 the school was presenting two productions a year and crowds had to be turned away from some performances.

Sir Eugene Goosens 1948 - 1955

There was nothing ordinary about Eugene Goosens. When he took up his appointment as director of the Conservatorium he was paid more than the prime minister of the day – an annual salary of 7000 pounds.

Goosens was an outstanding musician and it was he who campaigned for an Opera House and got it. He persuaded the then-premier Joe Cahill to build an opera house and to locate it at Bennelong Point, when others were suggesting it be built above Wynyard Railway station.

In a July 1952 issue of the newsletter *Canon*, Goosens wrote an article titled *Reflections*: "Unless Sydney gets an all-purpose opera house very

soon, the goal of higher performance standards will be negated for lack of a suitable show-window to display our orchestral, operatic, choral and ballet activities."

In a discussion of modern music, Goosens pointed out that anything different is difficult to accept at first. "Mussolini is said to favour an adage, 'it is necessary to live dangerously', which those who practise music and those who listen to it alike might adopt to advantage. In other words, rather than retire into the safe and smugly-complacent cell of self-righteousness… let us go out into the open, and make up our minds that we are finally going to tackle this hydra-headed monster of modernism."

Goosens' career in Australia came to an ignominious end in 1956, a few months after he was charged with importing banned goods (including pornography) into the country. He had come to the attention of the Vice Squad the previous year for his association with the "Witch of Kings Cross", the artist Rosaleen Norton. Whatever the truth may be about Goosens' involvement in Norton's satanic cult, the resulting public scandal, rumours that his downfall might have been set up, and his subsequent flight from Australia were a low point and a loss for Sydney's music community.

Bernard Heinze 1957 – 1966

By the time Heinze became director, musical standards were flourishing. The Conservatorium was glad to have an Australian-born director and if student newsletters are anything to go by there was a real buzz about the place. *Con-Script Op. I No. II,* a student newsletter published in December 1964, describes the director as "chief stallion of the stables" and the buffet as "the hall of learning".

Heinze believed music to be uplifting and that it was important for the moral good. By the age of 35 he was supervising the ABC's studio orchestras and by 1934 he had become the organisation's musical advisor. When he became director of the Conservatorium he was 65 and an obsessive collector, with over four million stamps and a dozen grandfather clocks to his name.

A lecturer's studio c.1916

Studio of Woodwind Chair, 2004

Heinze continued to conduct while he was director, reaching an arrangement with the ABC to conduct 40 orchestral concerts and 15 schools concerts per year. He was organised and disciplined by all accounts and arrived at work every day at 9am. Juggling these roles and managing an enormous amount of growth without any significant changes, especially to the building, were among his many challenges.

Perhaps not surprisingly there were hints of administrative chaos at the Conservatorium during his time, such as library books being stacked in boxes or in dusty bookcases lining the corridors.

Joseph Post 1966 - 1971

"Post continued the pathway forward that Heinze had set," John Painter reflected in 2004. "'I remember Post as an efficient director, a nice man who took an interest in the students."

The first director to have graduated from the Conservatorium, Post shared Heinze's philosophy that its role was to produce teachers and performers rather than theorists. A child prodigy, he had won a scholarship to the Conservatorium aged nine and he joined the State Orchestra as an oboist four years later.

Post worked as a conductor for the ABC from 1932 and conducted the Sydney and Melbourne Symphony Orchestras and the Australian Elizabethan Theatre Opera Company. Many of Heinze's plans came to fruition under Post: alterations to the building, the first full-time salaried teachers, a resident string quartet, the music education section coming under the Conservatorium's complete control and gaining status as a College of Advanced Education.

Painter's wife, cellist Lois Simpson, remembers Post as a disciplined musician. "I was appointed by Joe Post to teach cello at the Con. He was a major in the army before he conducted, and his behaviour on the rostrum was rather like that."

When Post conducted the first concert of the ABC subscription series for the Sydney Symphony Orchestra in 1966, *The Sydney Morning*

Herald described him as having a "constant sense of concentrated, unruffled alertness".

"There is practically no gesture in this conductor to distract the audience from the music… he knows how to bond the orchestra together, how to give them breathing space, yet keep their pulse taut" (*The Sydney Morning Herald,* March 10, 1966).

Rex Hobcroft 1972 - 1982

"Exciting" is the word that appears constantly when one reads about Hobcroft's time as director.

Always ready to explore new avenues, he encouraged Don Burrows in his quest to introduce jazz to the Con and took the institution into the age of electronics. He promoted music research and it was under his directorship that the Con's focus shifted to tertiary students.

American Howie Smith came to Australia to set up the jazz department and fellow American flautist James Pellerite was an artist in residence for a few months. Both of these moves reflected Hobcroft's commitment to establishing a visiting artists' program. Composer Martin Wesley-Smith helped set up the Electronic Music Studio, which was held in high regard around the country.

In 1973 there were more than 120 concerts performed at the Con, thanks to Hobcroft's enthusiasm. In the same year the Sydney Opera House opened and a collaborative relationship was formed with the Australian Opera Studio, whereby Con students were allowed to use practice rooms in the Opera House.

Vibrant personalities abounded during this time, including pianist Roger Woodward and conductors Richard Gill and Myer Fredman. John Painter and Robert Pikler established the Sydney Conservatorium Chamber Orchestra which later became the Australian Chamber Orchestra. A resident string quartet led by Carl Pini was formed and by 1978, international artists including Pinchas Zukerman, Itzhak Perlman, Yehudi Menuhin and Alfred Brendel had visited the Con, helping to make its reputation as *the* place to be for music students.

John Painter 1982 - 1985

Already an established cellist, Painter took over the directorship from Hobcroft, continuing the tradition of the performer-director. He had been principal cellist of the Sydney Symphony Orchestra for a number of years before he left to found the Sydney String Quartet.

"When Hobcroft came along the Whitlam Government made the Con part of the higher education sector, so salaries jumped up and the government was allowed to create more scholarships," Painter explained of the era preceding his appointment, during which funding for the arts was increased.

"Students could stay as long as they liked in the diploma course, as long as they paid their fees."

Part of Painter's role at the Conservatorium when he started the quartet was teaching for 15 hours a week. "We also rehearsed for three hours every day. I enjoyed teaching and I was chair of strings ~ I was really the first student advisor in my spare time. The students needed to talk to someone, and I helped them with their problems... I took the view that anything they were trying to do, I could do or had already been through."

Painter reflected that he had been fortunate to have the opportunity of being brought up in "the engine room". "I did everything, played in dance bands, quartets, commercial radio ~ I was playing in the Adelaide Symphony at 14... If I had the opportunity to do chamber music, I grabbed it, I didn't think about getting paid."

After three years in the director's chair, Painter left the Conservatorium to head the Canberra School of Music.

John Hopkins 1986 - 1991

Combining a love of music with a passion for education, John Hopkins became director of the Con in 1986. A practising musician, Hopkins continued his association with the Auckland Philharmonic Orchestra and his role as artistic advisor to the Sydney Symphony Orchestra. He headed the ABC's Music Department from 1963 to 1973 and took the innovative step of introducing prom concerts during this time.

"In those prom concerts we introduced Australian audiences to composers like Messiaen, Lutoslawski... also Australian composers, Richard Meale, Nigel Butterley and Don Banks."

A sandstone cistern in the foreground unearthed during the re-development excavation, located on the second level of the atrium

Endless meetings to discuss the Conservatorium's amalgamation with Sydney University consumed a lot of Hopkins' time but the plan came to fruition during his directorship. "All four [Sydney] universities were vying to get us and there were lots of meetings. Once the University of Sydney was decided upon a lot of time was spent going to the uni ~ just getting there took ages."

Both Hopkins and his successor, Ronald Smart, assumed numerous roles during this transition period, and their job descriptions were just as varied. They were known as directors and then as principals and by the time Sharman Pretty arrived, the position was formally that of Dean of the Conservatorium.

An experienced conductor, Hopkins had come to the Conservatorium with the understanding that there would be a new building and funding for visiting artists and Baroque studies. Although the new building came much later, he did succeed in getting the Joseph Post Auditorium rebuilt.

Hopkins also helped set up the Sydney Conservatorium of Music Foundation in 1987.

Ronald Smart 1992 - 1994

Elevating the diploma course to degree status was one of Dr Ronald Smart's many achievements during his period at the Conservatorium. Changing roles at various times (head of practical studies, principal, acting director), Dr Smart was a passionate music educator.

The first Australian to study classical music at an American university, he broke new ground in many areas at the Conservatorium when he returned to Australia in 1974 equipped with a doctorate from the University of Southern California.

"When we changed the DSCM [Diploma of the State Conservatorium of Music] course to a bachelor of music and introduced a master's degree, the whole status of the Con changed," he said. "It immediately became a recognised institution, offering a university degree. It gave the Con a whole different perspective internationally."

A glimpse of the city through the library skylight

A student on the way to an Alexander Technique class

With over two years' experience as a trombonist in the Sydney Symphony Orchestra under Eugene Goosens and Joseph Post, Dr Smart understood the demands of being a performing musician. He was the second Con graduate to become director, the first having been Post. "Joseph Post was a good friend to me when I was in the Sydney Symphony ~ he conducted a number of my concerto performances… But my motivation was to be an educator. I spent my time well in the orchestra, studying how the conductors operated and so on."

These skills came to the fore when Dr Smart revitalised the Conservatorium Symphony Orchestra. Two major tours were organised: a 1982 state-funded trip to China and a 1985 federally-funded trip to the United States. "We opened the Memphis May Festival and Richard Tognetti performed the Tchaikovsky Concerto."

Another innovation was "Orchestra weeks" ~ "We conducted the week as though the orchestra was a professional orchestra, and had conductors such as Mackerras come in. Eventually we forged a relationship with the Opera House and each year we did a big orchestral/choral performance."

The Conservatorium Chorale was Dr Smart's other passion. He took this group on a one-month tour of Asia, developing international relationships for the Con.

Working closely with the state government in an effort to resolve where best to locate the Conservatorium. Dr Smart thought that it should move to Rozelle in Sydney's inner west. "As soon as Bob Carr was elected [as Premier] the first thing he did was to cancel the move to Rozelle. He thought it should stay in the city… I [now] think the new building is stunning. It's a world-class institution."

Dr Smart was responsible for commissioning a history of the Conservatorium, *Sounds from the Stables*. It was written by Dianne Collins and published in 2001.

Views of the library

Sharman Pretty 1995 - 2003

An accomplished businesswoman, Sharman Pretty's major achievement was to secure funding to redevelop the Con into the world-class building that it is today.

Pretty, an oboist, had worked her way through various roles before being appointed director of the Con in 1995. Proving herself in her role as manager of Youth Music Australia and the Australian Youth Orchestra Pretty was already well-versed in attracting funding.

The redevelopment of the Conservatorium was so impressive a project that NSW Government architect Chris Johnson and architectural firm Daryl Jackson, Robin Dyke and Robert Tanner won an Australia Award of Merit for Urban Design Excellence in 2002.

Satisfying a number of clients and stakeholders was no easy task but a necessary one for the redevelopment to be a success. There had been the Con itself to consider, as well as the high school, the university, the state government, the Royal Botanic Gardens, the students, lobby groups and consent authorities such as State Rail, National Trust, Sydney City Council, Heritage Council, Central Sydney Planning Committee and four architectural players.

The budget for the job was set at 69 million dollars but blew out eventually to 144 million.

The Daily Telegraph described the renovation as "Mission Impossible" (August 25, 2001) "Your job, should you choose to accept it, is to combine a high school and a university, an archaeological dig, four recital halls, a high-rise office tower, a railway line rumbling through the middle of it, and make it invisible."

If there was anyone who could overcome these obstacles it was Sharman Pretty. Scouring the world, she contracted Chicago-based Kirkegaard and Associates, acousticians whose former projects included The Barbican Centre and the Royal Festival Hall in London. Architect Daryl Jackson had designed the Canberra School of Music, which Pretty had attended as a student and also as a teacher.

The resulting new building features more than 70 practice rooms, a refurbished Verbrugghen Hall, two recital halls, a café that is used as an informal performing space and a well-equipped library.

Combining old and new, the archaeological findings uncovered during excavation are featured in a museum-like display as one enters the Conservatorium. The foundations of the old Verbrugghen Hall can be seen in all their glory. Initial construction work also uncovered part of a road that dated back to the 1820s as well as fragments of a convict drain. These too have been incorporated into the new foyer

The decision to keep the Conservatorium in the city was controversial at the time. However, it is unlikely that such a spectacular building would have resulted had the Con moved to Rozelle. While the decision to restore the premises was fraught with challenges, the Con's prestigious setting in the Royal Botanic Gardens, within sight of the Opera House and in walking distance of the city, ensures that it remains a focal point in Sydney's artistic life.

" The thing that impressed me when I first walked into the Conservatorium was the way that sunlight soaks through the glass panels creating a feeling of space in the main atrium. This is even more surprising when you remind yourself that most of the building is underground. "

Shelley Jamison, a postgraduate viola student

Brass

Andrew Evans

Chair, Brass Unit

Employing the staff from whom he would like to learn has been the key to creating a good brass department for trumpeter Andrew Evans.

"The staff I employ have an excellent combination of pedagogical skills and still have that passion for their instrument. They also have a great work ethic and a good sense of humour."

Evans has had extensive experience as a professional musician, including an international career of renown. "I had some fantastic teachers – I learned with two guys in the Tasmanian Symphony orchestra. One of them was like a dad and taught me for nothing. He was a very committed, musical man. I love him a lot."

After gaining a position in the ABC training orchestra in Sydney, during which time he studied with Sydney Symphony principal trumpet Daniel Mendelow, Evans won a job in the Western Australian Symphony Orchestra. Thereafter this accomplished musician was awarded an opportunity to perform internationally at the highest level: "I won a German Government scholarship and went to Berlin. I studied with the first trumpeter in the Berlin Philharmonic and he invited me to do some off-stage trumpet with them for their last concert with Von Karajan. I did some more concerts with them after that and it was a very positive experience."

Evans has also performed in shows since moving to Melbourne. "I thought I would last two weeks but I learned to play the trumpet during that time, having to be spot on every time." Still an active performer, he often asks his students to play gigs with him so they gain professional experience.

"I feel very privileged – I've struck a good balance [between teaching and playing]. It's almost a sanctuary to go in and teach."

A full compliment of the brass section

Trumpet student Caitlin Shehan warming up before going into a rehearsal

Brass ensemble practising in the Verbrugghen Hall

"The staff I employ have an excellent combination of pedagogical skills and still have that passion for their instrument... they also have a great work ethic and a good sense of humour."

Andrew Evans, Chair of Brass Unit

Brass ensemble playing from another area in the same hall

Students preparing for a practice session

Neil Ryan playing the trombone

Choir

Brahms' Ein Deutsches Requiem Op 45 being performed in the Verbrugghen Hall

Neil McEwan conducting Mozart's Requiem

Neil McEwan in a choir practice session

Student Cassandra Brennan singing in the Sydney Conservatorium choir

Composition / Musicology

Michael Smetanin

Chair, Composition Unit

Not many composers can say they've almost inspired industrial action but Michael Smetanin is one who boasts this dubious honour. His work *Black Snow* was considered so outrageous that symphony musicians in Melbourne and Sydney threatened industrial action.

That was in 1997. Smetanin was appointed Chair of the Composition Unit two years ago but has been teaching at the Conservatorium since 1998.

Of *Black Snow*, he said simply, "It caused a huge scandal; the orchestras didn't want to play it ~ it's a pretty aggressive piece." When asked why he scored *Black Snow* for such a large and loud orchestra, he replied, "Because I wanted to write a big piece. I could have taken it further ~ it wasn't that overboard, but it did get new music on the front page of newspapers at the time."

Fellow composer Andrew Ford wrote in *The Sydney Morning Herald* about the reaction that it was a shame Smetanin wasn't French. "They really know what to do with a *succès de scandale*. You repeat it," Ford wrote. But *Black Snow* has not been performed since.

With a string of awards to his name Smetanin describes his compositions as "music with attitude. It's relatively discordant; I like to make unusual sounds that have some fetching quality."

Lewis Cornwall

Chair, Musicology Unit

Bringing the world of harmony alive is the passion of musicologist and oboist Lewis Cornwall. Joining the staff of the Con in 1982 to tutor in harmony, he gained a full-time position in 1989.

"I like harmony to be thought of as understanding the mechanisms of tonal music ~ the why of it all. Understanding the choices composers have made, why some formulas and voice-leading work and others don't."

Working with the repertoire is a focus of his teaching and essential to bringing the world of harmony alive. "Ravel wasn't particularly proud of *Bolero* ~ it breaks all the rules and he thought it was a bit crude. As soon as you introduce a piece from the real world it doesn't necessarily follow all the rules... I find it amusing when students come and say, 'Am I allowed to do this?' when the point is, will it sound good?"

Every student is different and Cornwall often finds that students develop a deeper appreciation of harmony as they mature. "[Assistant Principal] Peter McCallum said harmony is a bit like religion, you come to it later in life. It's so true ~ harmony students come back after graduation and say they're interested in counterpoint."

The musicology unit also teaches music history and aural studies among other subjects. An active composer, Cornwall was a founding member of Music Performed, which organised new-music workshops for young composers.

Richard Toop

Former Chair, Musicology Unit

Many musicians who have graduated from the Sydney Conservatorium will have experienced the might of Richard Toop's intellect. Famous for lecturing from memory ("because I know it"), his lectures positively burst at the seams with information.

Chair of the Musicology Unit from 1981 to 2001, Toop now holds the esteemed title of Reader. Specialising in contemporary music, with a sideline for late Beethoven, Toop's interest in music started when he was 14. "I made up my mind to listen to all this weird-sounding stuff ~ Berg's opera *Wozzeck* and things like that ~ and I decided, I'm not going to let it beat me," he said simply.

"One day I was with my parents in Devon… There was an ensemble of students from the Royal College of Music rehearsing Messiaen's *L'Oiseaux Exotiques* of 1958. I asked to spend the summer holidays there, so there I was, aged 16, sitting in on classes with Berio, Maderna, Lutoslawski… I loved the whole world of the whole thing."

Completing a Bachelor of Arts at the Northern University in England, Toop got jobs as a German translator while also working as a pianist. "I translated a bunch of Stockhausen's essays from German and got to meet Stockhausen in 1969… eventually I became his teaching assistant."

In the meantime the Conservatorium was looking for a junior lecturer.
"Roger Woodward recommended me to John Painter who was deputy director to Rex Hobcroft at the time."

Understanding more than just the notes is important for any musician and this is the reason why musicology is vital, Toop believes. "It's essential to understand where music sits in a cultural context. Having a basic literacy and understanding of harmony and being able to hear ~ musicians should be able to hear. I don't think that's too outrageous a thing to say."

Introducing modern music courses has been one of Toop's passions. "I proposed a course with a smaller proportion of art music and a large proportion of popular music, and then one that offered the reverse. Years ago I started a seminar called Radical Rock. It's still going and now needs to be divided into two classes."

Toop has contributed to the *Grove Dictionary of Opera*, the *New Revised Grove* and the *Cambridge History of 20ᵗʰ Century Music*. He has been published in international journals such as *The Musical Quarterly* and the *Neue Zeitschrift für Musik*. His monograph on Ligeti was published by Phaidon Press (London) in 1999.

Musicology student David Griffin conducting a student's composition

"There's a lot more art to maths than people imagine. The music came along before all the rules came along, and the theorists are usually lagging behind."

Lewis Cornwall, Chair of Musicology Unit

Student Mikhaela Adam playing the marimba

Sandy Sin playing the gamelan

"I write music with attitude - discordant and unusual sounds that have some fetching quality."

Michael Smetanin, Chair of Composition

Ensemble Studies

David Miller

Chair, Ensemble Studies

If David Miller isn't at a keyboard he's probably at home asleep or eating a meal. Music is his life.

"I've seen a lot of changes over 25 years. I was first here as a lecturer in accompaniment." Head of the chamber music department since 1995, Miller said "accompaniment is the first level of chamber music, it requires a special temperament. It's difficult when students are brought up as soloists ~ anywhere in a career they will have to work as an ensemble or in a chamber orchestra".

Clashes between students sometimes take place during coaching sessions. "I have to referee some of the clashes, where there are differences of opinion and different senses of responsibility. For example, one person won't turn up or they come unprepared," Miller said.

Encouraging students to think for themselves and broadening their views is important to Miller, however. "Here students are taught to forge their own ideas, draw on other people's opinions and form something that is unique to that group."

Miller said the Con now has an accompaniment department, "[which is] unique in this country ~ experienced accompanists who are able to coach an ensemble and help with the preparation of recitals. Other institutions provide financial assistance to get someone in to help students prepare".

The increasing number of overseas students at the Con has a particular impact on ensemble studies. "We get cultural differences [that affect performance]. One girl doing chamber music is used to playing with her sister ~ she's older so always has been the dominant one, because that is appropriate in her culture."

Miller credits his past teachers with giving him everything he needed to make it as a professional musician. "Good teachers are rare beings… they set you on the right path."

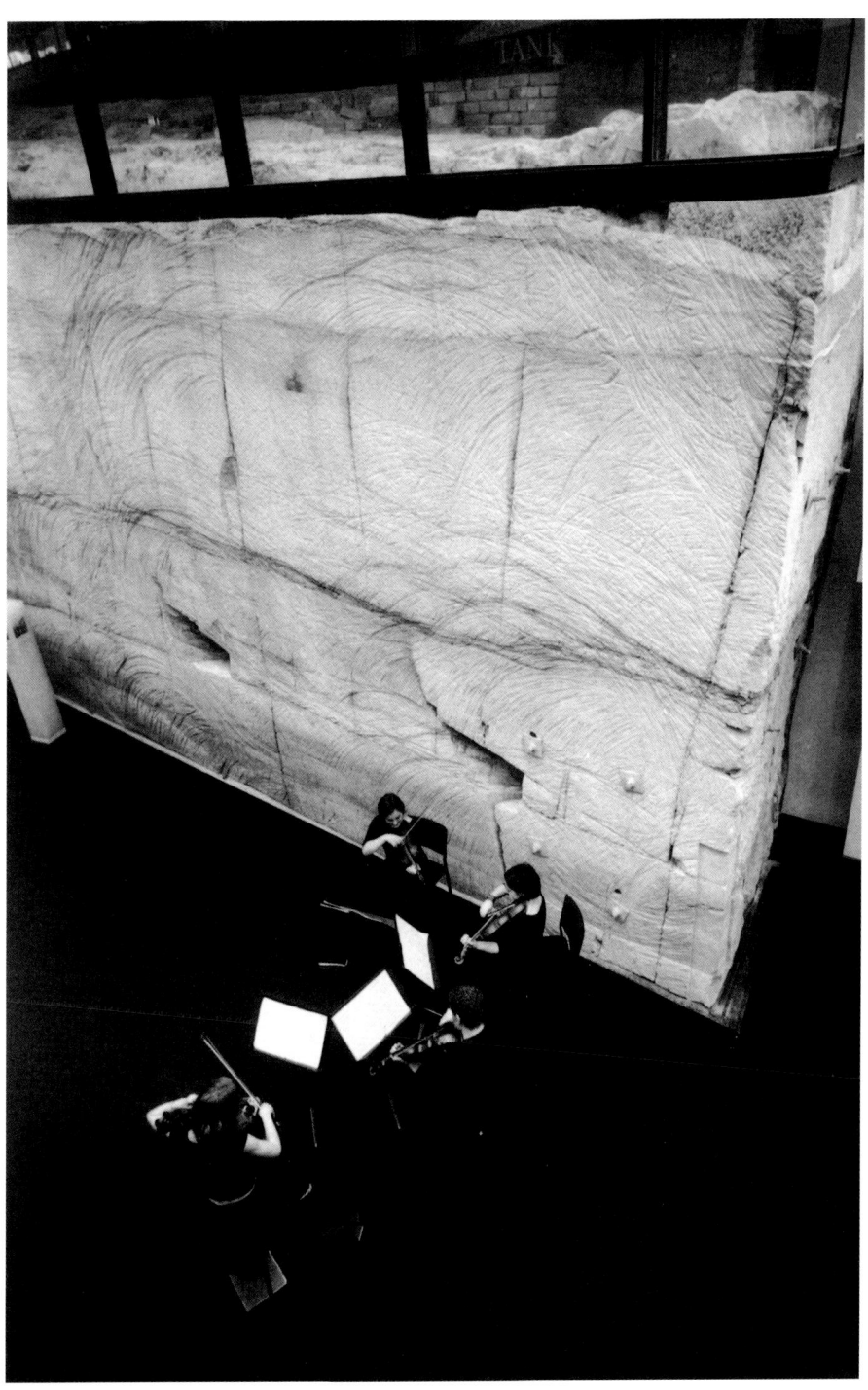

A student string quartet practising in the atrium before a concert.

An ensemble giving a lunch-time concert

" Empathy to me is someone who can whisper a Wagner leitmotif in your ear."

Composer James Easton

Another ensemble in performance

" Music is my life. It's my background, it's my world. I love music and I love musicians.
I understand their plight."

Rachel Whealy, a former Conservatorium student, is a cellist and founder of the
chamber music group, the Bravura Ensemble

Ensemble Chair David Miller teaching Claire Kahn (left) and Marie Searles (right)

Jazz

Richard Montz

Former Chair, Jazz Unit

Receiving a phone call at 3am from a student at a jam session was one of the worst moments in Dick Montz's life. "[Some students] called me and said another student had collapsed and asked me what to do," Montz said.

"They called me first! I told them to call the ambulance and a doctor and so on. It turned out the student had died from an aneurism in the brain."

The bond between teacher and student is a professional relationship that inevitably becomes personal and crosses into life after hours. "When I first started the job I asked about the hours per week. I was told, 'You do the job until it's done' by Ron Smart. Spending hours on the phone counselling students is just part of the job."

The jazz unit is fondly known among staff and students as the "ghetto". "We're down in the dungeons and we're like our own miniature music school here," Montz said. "We have brass, wind, strings, percussion, theory, aural ~ we cover all the disciplines that the classical people do, with a jazz flavour."

"Good jazz musicians need an excellent ear, a love of jazz and the creative ability to improvise… and they have to be 'unique'. Jazz has survived on newness."

Organising and marketing their own gigs is part of the jazz musician's role: "[Jazz musicians] are mainly freelance players and have to be driven to survive adversity."

Montz was the first person to complete a Masters of Music degree at the Conservatorium in 1986. "The jazz course has gone from two years to a full degree program. Students do a Bachelor of Music with a jazz major and there's a two year Masters by research in jazz."

Jazz teacher Dick Montz trying out a piece in his studio

"Good Jazz musicians need an excellent ear, a love of jazz and the creative ability to improvise - they must understand the harmony of the songs they're working with - and they have to be unique or unusual."

Dick Montz, former Chair of Jazz Unit

Dick Montz (right) conducting the Big Band

Big Band No.1 in action, under the baton of Dick Montz

Student Michael Rivett performing with the Big Band No. 1 in the Music Café

Jazz drum student James Cameron in rehearsal

Keyboard

Elizabeth Powell

Chair, Keyboard Unit

Elizabeth Powell studied with Claudio Arrau and with teachers who were intimate friends with Debussy, Ravel, Brahms and Mahler. She calls herself a fossil and admits that when she came to Sydney at the age of 37 she thought it was "a bit of a musical desert".

The pianist turned 70 in 2004 and has seen eight directors come and go since starting at the Con under Joseph Post. "I met Joseph through mutual friends ~ he was a very interesting man, and he used to come into the teaching studios. He took an active interest. There isn't time for a director to do that now, there are too many people."

Post advised Powell that there was no teaching work available. But within 10 days she was asked to fill in for Isadore Goodman, who had to go back to South Africa for three months to see his mother who was dying. "After three months Post said, 'we'd like you to stay' ~ the rest is history".

Still an active performer, Powell enjoys her teaching because she "gets more out of it". "I love being able to see the students change, to see a result over the years. I'm giving something to a human being and they take it and shape it. You hope you're giving them food for their future."

Now that the Conservatorium is part of Sydney University the one-on-one lessons could be under threat. Powell said students were perhaps unaware of how lucky they were to have such a privilege. "The university is about classes. In most courses like nursing, medicine or law, it's about group lectures. It's a privilege having private lessons, and it costs such a lot."

Elizabeth Powell in her studio, teaching Yvonne Kuan

"I'm giving something to human beings and they take it and shape it. You hope you're giving them food for their future."

Elizabeth Powell, Chair of Keyboard Unit

Student Rachael Lin practising, with fellow student Ludwig E. Sugiri in the background

"Music makes me nervous, music challenges me and music makes me feel beautiful"

Rachel Lin, a piano final year student

Belinda McGlynn at the piano in the Recital Hall

David Miller coaching Marie Searles

Gerard Willems

Keyboard Unit

Dutch-born Gerard Willems believes in a holistic approach to teaching. "I was brought up in the Dutch choral tradition ~ I was in a choir at the age of eight and we sang Bach's St Matthew Passion every year."

"Many students only think with their fingers, but it's important to sing in a choir, to do chamber music, to get exposure to other instruments… so they become all-round musicians who can hear music with their inner ear."

Included in this overall view is relating music to the world at large, especially nature. Being on the doorstep of the Royal Botanic Gardens is something Willems uses to inspire a greater understanding of natural beauty in his students.

"There are as many Beethoven sonata interpretations as there are blades of grass," he said. "I tell my students this and they go to the gardens with a different view."

The Conservatorium's historic location helps to link the past with the present, Willems believes. "We're dealing with a lot of history in the past when we play music. Understanding history and how we fit into it all is part of growing up. Beauty does not have to be re-invented. I see us as perpetuating that magic of that mysterious thing called beauty."

He reflects that the student-teacher relationship has changed over the years. "When I was a student, the teacher was the pinnacle of respect. Now students expect respect to be earned by the teacher."

The new building has improved morale and communication between staff and students. "The building has brought everyone together. It's wonderful to be able to run into each other in the corridors; usually good ideas come about from casual contacts… [like] ideas for concert programs. It's made a big difference in the community at the Con."

Gerard Willems teaching four students in a piano master class, as they play a Mozart Symphony on two keyboards

Piano accompaniment student Philippa Cook playing a piece on the harpsichord

"Music education is about loving music so I changed the focus of the course from being entirely on classroom teaching to any kind of teaching - children, old people, disabled kids - anyone."

Peter Dunbar-Hall, Chair of Music Education

Judy Bailey teaching blind piano student Scott Erichsen

Organ lecturer Philip Swanton looking on while Sarah Kim
plays Thalben-Ball's piece for pedal only

Emma Rose practising

Orchestral Studies

Harry Spence Lyth

Chair, Conducting Unit

Harry Spence Lyth has been conductor in residence and Sesqui Lecturer in Conducting at the Conservatorium since 2002. After completing initial studies in the natural sciences at Cambridge University, Lyth studied conducting at the Conservatorium Giuseppe Verdi in Milan and at the Mozarteum in Salzburg.

"I got the opera bug when I went to Italy," he said. "I've always preferred opera, it's more intimate... I love conducting, I love the repertoire, I love the orchestra as an instrument as it has so many possibilities."

Lyth has worked throughout Europe. Now based in Australia, raising the standard of the Conservatorium Orchestra is his primary mission. "I'm trying to increase the profile of the orchestra in the community. There's a lot of inverted snobbery in the media towards the Conservatorium Orchestra - they ignore us."

Lyth lived in Berlin for 25 years, where there are seven orchestras. "Sydney has a sparse cultural landscape - there's only one [major] orchestra."

Improving the conducting course at the Con is another goal as students are unable to major in conducting. "I'm re-designing the course, but we need funding," Lyth said. "We need what we call 'podium time'. This involves conducting students having access to professional orchestras. If you learn to conduct with a bad orchestra, you become a bad conductor."

Lyth stresses the importance of conductors at the grass-roots level. "The community needs a lot of conductors, they're catalysts for society. They start choirs, it's not just an ego trip."

Harry Spence Lyth taking the baton in a rehearsal

Conducting student Cathy Chan trying out her skills

Cello student Johanna Fluhrer in an orchestral rehearsal

"Studying conducting at the Con has been great for meeting other would-be conductors and discussing ideas. Normally conducting is a pretty solitary experience."

Cathy Chan

Another conducting student Jade Tinkler

Lecturer Russell Hammond conducting

The Sydney Conservatorium Symphony at a lunchtime concert led by a student

The same symphony orchestra
during a performance prior to
the 1997 re-development
(*Picture courtesy of the
Conservatorium Library*)

Brian Chen concentrating on his cello playing

"I believe music to be very healing. Visualising a positive outcome and seeing myself playing the way I wanted to was really helpful…many musicians don't like to admit to being vulnerable to performance nerves, but it's a fact of life."

Violinist Kirsten Williams, Sydney Symphony Orchestra associate concertmaster and a graduate of the Conservatorium

Harry Spence Lyth teaching a conducting class, with students Natalie Jacobs and Simon Thew looking on

"A conductor's medium is all about coordinating gesture, posture and spirit in order to give justice to what the music is saying, and being a psychological metronome, but without beating the music at the players."

Natalie Jacobs, a student of Graduate Diploma in Performance (Conducting)

Conducting student Daniel Smith and other students being taught baton technique

Simon Thew on the podium

"Conducting is not about beating the value of a quaver. It's what we do in the space of it in the context of the music."

Alan Ho

Students (from left to right) Martin Andrews, Cassandra Brennan and Alan Ho revising
their baton techniques over lunchtime

Percussion

Daryl Pratt

Chair, Percussion Unit

Diversity is the word that comes to mind regarding percussionist Daryl Pratt. He left the United States to join the faculty at the Canberra School of Music, where he stayed for six years. Pratt, who holds a Master's degree in performance from the University of Southern California, moved to Sydney in 1991.

"When I first arrived in Australia I found that the departments were disconnected - that was something I hadn't experienced in the States," he said. "I have a diverse background and teach a few composition classes and have a student in the jazz department."

Admitting that percussionists are probably the most likely of instrumentalists to cross over from classical to jazz, Pratt described his interests as classical, jazz and world music. "The percussion world is like one big family."

He believes diversity is essential to providing a range of employment opportunities. "[Former student] Richard Gleeson graduated from a music education degree and he works at about four different jobs - he works at a percussion shop, plays with the Australian Chamber Orchestra and Sydney Symphony when they need extra players, he plays in musicals and he teaches."

Two other graduates of Pratt's, Alison Eddington and Claire Edwardes, won the ABC Young Performers' Competition in 1995 and 2000 respectively, and have embarked on classical careers.

He says that the new Con has made life easier for percussionists. "We used to be on the third floor of the Pitt Street building and I walked up and down between that building and the Con two or three times a day - it was great for my fitness. I now have five dedicated studios and a big rehearsal room. These resources are really important for us."

Chiron Meller (left) learning the marimba with his teacher Daryl Pratt

"I have a diverse background and teach a few composition classes…I try to provide a platform that enables students to go in different directions, so they have diversity across a range of styles."

Daryl Pratt, Chair of Percussion Unit

Percussion student Chiron Meller playing the timpani in the Percussion Studio

Performance Outreach & Communication

Mark Walton teaching a student in Armidale by video link

"In three years time I hope to be able to point to a map of NSW and say, this is happening there next week…the future of music in Australia is in the hands of people at the grassroots level. I've encouraged a team of graduates to go out to the country, to immerse themselves in the community - it's a bit like a doctor moving to a country town."

Mark Walton, Chair of Performance Outreach and Communication Unit

Mark Walton

Chair, Performance Outreach & Communication Unit

Immersing musicians in society is the passion of clarinettist and saxophonist Mark Walton. "I was head of woodwind for a long time, but I'm always looking for new, exciting projects to work on. I've always had an interest in outreach."

English by birth, he moved to Australia after experiencing the "balmy weather" of Sydney during a residency at the Conservatorium after a tour as soloist with the New Zealand Symphony Orchestra.

His innovative work in bringing music to people in isolated areas is conducted by video-conferencing. He teaches students via video to give them support in areas where there may not be a teacher available, in person at least.

In doing this Walton is bringing music to people who would otherwise not have access to it, and building up an awareness of music in Australian society. "I'm concerned that music is only found in a thin layer of society in Australia. It's very difficult to get audiences unless there's a lot of media attention. I've encouraged a team of graduate students [from the Con] to go out to the country, live there and teach."

Walton encourages the graduate students to become "community" musicians.
"In three years time I want to be able to point to a map of NSW and say, this is happening there next week."

With students posted in Orange, Bathurst, Dubbo, Coonabarabran and Young, Walton is well on the way. The next step, he said, is asking the graduates who have set themselves up "out bush" to be mentors to new recruits.

The program's success has attracted sponsorship from Yamaha Australia, which publicises related news in a quarterly magazine that circulates around Australia and New Zealand.

Strings

Goetz Richter

Chair, Strings Unit

Diagnostic skills are what violinist Goetz Richter uses when he teaches. He likens teaching to being a doctor. "The students come and I tell them what they need to fix, it's like therapy."

Chair of the String Unit since 2002, Richter has been teaching at the Con since 1988. He held the position of associate concertmaster with the Sydney Symphony Orchestra until he became Chair of the unit. "I've been interested in teaching since I was a student," he said. "I tutored at National Music Camps for a few years and students started asking if they could study with me."

Approached by Sharman Pretty to become fractional head of department in 1997, Richter always believed the position should be full-time, as it has since become.

A father of two with pianist Dr Jeanelle Carrigan, he has always involved himself fully in everything he does. "In 2002 I made some changes in my life and I'm no longer a member of the orchestra, although I go back occasionally."

Passionate about preparing students for orchestral auditions, Richter holds lots of orchestral classes. His busy schedule includes teaching privately for up to 35 hours a week and coaching chamber musicians. "It's more exhausting than being in the orchestra. You spend more time thinking about other people's problems."

Richter combines his love of music with an overlapping passion for the history of philosophy, in which he has a degree. "We must know the past, we must transform it. If you are not cognisant of the past you can't recognise different styles."

Strings Chair Goetz Richter giving Bronwyn Turner a violin lesson

"The students come and I tell them what to fix - it's like therapy."

Goetz Richter, Chair of Strings Unit

Cello lecturer Georg Pedersen teaching and conducting a cello ensemble

"Learning the cello is an instrumental journey. It's a complicated instrument because every note can be played in 20 different ways."

Georg Pedersen, cello teacher

Violin lecturer Wanda Wilkomirska teaching post-graduate student Catherine Chartard

"I have studied in the Royal College of Music in London and also in Paris, but I find studying this year at the Con very exciting, with a lot of chance to perform as well."

Catherine Chartard, a postgraduate violin student.

Double bass students Anna Du (left) and Jacqueline Dossor relaxing between classes

Violin student George Zacharias tuning his violin in the atrium

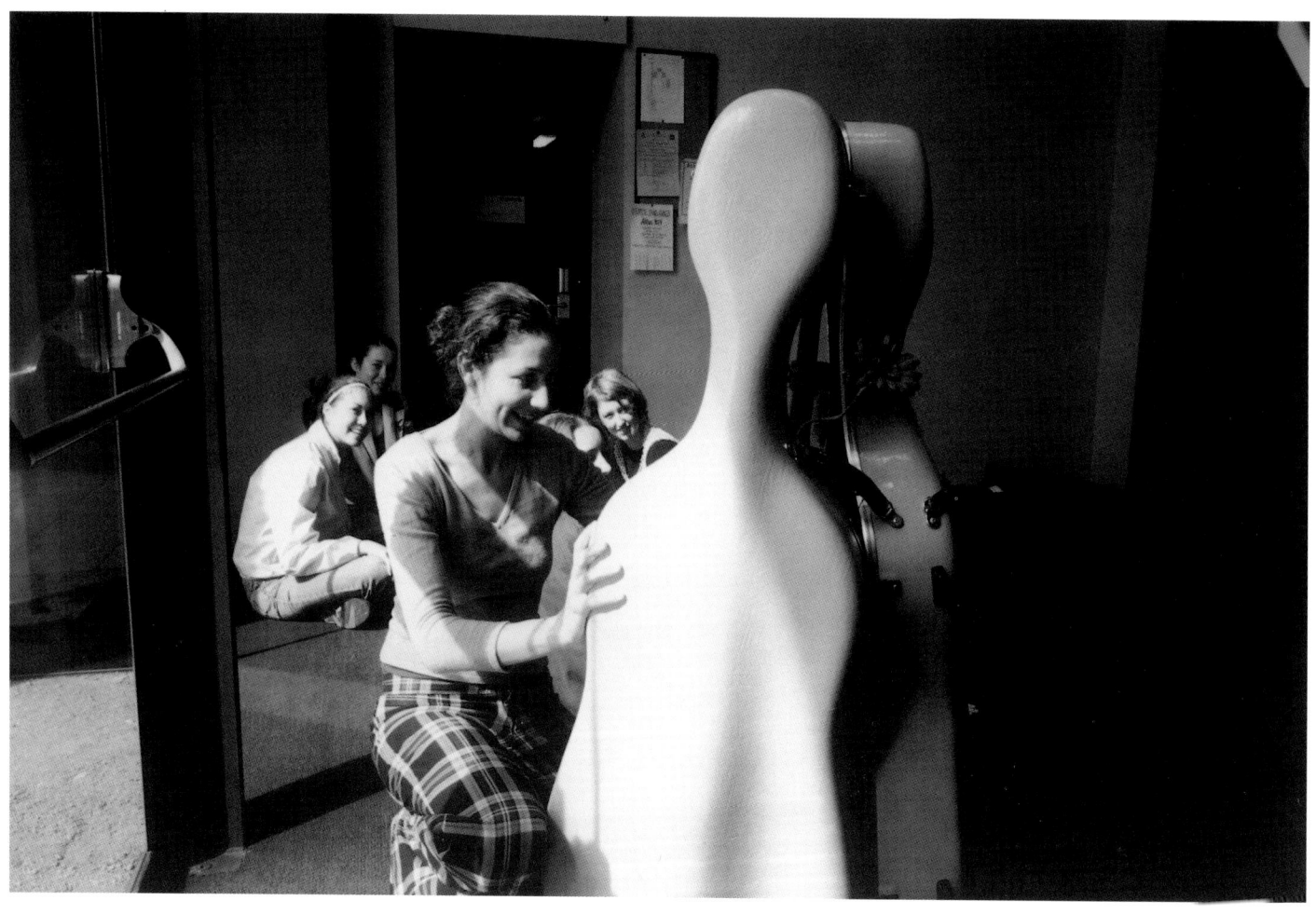

Students waiting to begin orchestra rehearsal

"I remember doing harmony in an old turret room, living with that wood, the smells, the sounds."

Megan Taylor, cellist and former Conservatorium High School student.

Double bass students Jacqueline Dossor (top) and Hayley Clare (bottom)

Viola student Luke Spicer in between rehearsals

Post-graduate harp student Amy Tam preparing an examination piece in the harp studio

A guitar student in one of the many practice rooms

"Gone are the days when you saw students practising in the gardens under a tree. We have 70-odd dedicated practice rooms now, and I have never seen them all used at the same time. This doesn't mean it doesn't happen."

Greg Pikler, guitar teacher

Voice / Opera

Michael Halliwell

Chair, Vocal Studies Unit

Improvising in German is all in a day's work for singer Michael Halliwell. "I was doing an operetta and had a dialogue scene with an American soprano. My German was not the best and neither was hers. We started the duet and the revolving door got stuck so we had to ad lib in a language we did not speak! It only lasted for about 10 seconds but it felt like a lifetime."

South-African born Halliwell joined the staff of the Conservatorium in 1995 after living and working in Europe for 15 years. He combined his interest in music and literature by completing a PhD on opera and the novel genre at the University of Natal in South Africa. "I looked at the process of adaptation, how the characters change, how the narrative undergoes transformations… [For example] when you look at an opera like *Hamlet,* written by Ambroise Thomas, it ends happily [as opposed to Shakespeare's drama]."

As a teacher, Halliwell enjoys the challenge of working with different singers and teaches all voice types. "It's stimulating and it makes you question yourself ~ no two students are the same."

Maree Ryan

Vocal Studies Unit

It's easy to believe that teaching is an artform when you speak to vocal teacher Maree Ryan. She likens teaching to an artist adding colour with a brush. "I like a sound that's bright, clear, but warm so it has depth and brilliance."

Sound has to be full of colour to be beautiful, according to Ryan. "When an artist picks up a brush and the painting looks too dark, you add brightness to it; if it's too light you add darkness… that's exactly what I do with the voice.

"Renee Fleming and Kiri te Kanawa have the *squillo* ~ this is Italian for ping and has a lot to do with the resonance in the sound. Opera singers don't have a microphone so we have to carry."

Ryan has been teaching at the Conservatorium for 20 years and is in the coveted position of being one of three vocal teachers that Opera Australia recommends to young students.

More than 50 of her students have made the finals of competitive national singing competitions. "One of my students won the Mathy singing competition [the Marianne Mathy Singing Scholarship is worth 30,000 dollars].

"Teaching these kinds of students is a bit like being Ian Thorpe's swimming coach ~ this student's parents told me they did a lot of research before they came to me. They decided they liked the sound I produced and within a year she'd won a major competition… it can make all the difference between having a career and having none, so it's a very serious business."

Many of her former students come back for regular "tune-up" lessons. "It's like tuning a Porsche. They want ears that they can trust."

Voice lecturer Maree Ryan working with soprano Tanith Bryce

"Choosing the right teacher can make all the difference between having a career and having none, so it's a very serious business... building a reputation as a teacher takes many years of significant contributions. If you don't produce students of quality, no one wants to study with you."

Maree Ryan, vocal teacher

Italian language lecturer Nicole Dorigo coaching Greg Mcleod to sing correctly in Italian

Nicole Dorigo demonstrating finesse in vocal production

"Collegiality is what the profession is all about. It's important to be disciplined, to have self-respect...I get really emotional about music - I say to my students, ' Where's your heart? Haven't you got emotions?

Sharolyn Kimmorley, Chair of Opera Unit

Sharolyn Kimmorley

Chair, Opera Unit

"Energising" is the way Sharolyn Kimmorley describes coaching. Having worked at Opera Australia as a vocal coach for 28 years, she joined the ranks of the Conservatorium in 2000. Combining a strong commitment to her students with an undying passion for music makes Kimmorley a great asset.

"I love it, I adore it, the kids are here because they want to be ~ they're not jaded and it's great to be able to contribute to their development."

Kimmorley's role as vocal coach involves many different facets, including sound production, breathing, presentation, interpretation, style, vowel sounds, singing in different languages, diction and creating characterisation through the text.

"I ask students, 'what do you want this music to tell you, what do you want to say? Why? If you want to be able to engage in a dialogue, have a reason'."

Despite being paid a part-time salary she works more than a full-time load. "I get such joy out of it. I'm lucky; I'm earning my living doing what I love."

Professional singing is challenging, especially in opera. "Students have to want a living as an opera singer more than anything else; it's very difficult to get work. Many go off to work abroad. They have to open their minds, have the passion, the sense of inquiry."

"As a teacher I always have to have the antennas up so I can see if anything is wrong," Kimmorley said. "You have to be honest, you have to be positive, and I always want to work through the issues with students if they're having a difficult time."

Dress rehearsal of The Marriage of Figaro with the chorus in Act One

Marcelline, on learning the person she has wanted to marry is in fact Figaro, her son (centre left and right Erin O'Connor and Greg Mcleod), with producer Patrick Nolan (left) and Alexander Freeman (right) looking on

Susanna and Figaro (Kathy Grotty and Greg Mcleod) in a moment of elation in The Marriage of Figaro

The Count (Gavin Lockley) flirting with everyone

"Sometimes a student will pose a question that you can't answer and I don't try to kid the students that I can answer everything…I try to instil independence and responsibility in my students. It's a tough life being a singer, glamorous but very competitive."

Michael Halliwell, Chair of Vocal Unit

Singers Florian Crumm (centre) and Javier Vilarino (right) in the Wedding Scene of the opera

A dance scene in The Marriage of Figaro, with Emily Garth and Tanith
Bryce (top left and right) and Rebecca Hilder (bottom centre)

Woodwind

Andrew Barnes

Chair, Woodwind Unit

Most people don't expect an economics graduate to end up earning a living as a highly acclaimed professional musician.

However, this is just what bassoonist Andrew Barnes has done. Barnes, who graduated with an economics degree from Macquarie University, returned home to Sydney after an absence of 10 years to take up the position of head of the Con's woodwind unit.

Explaining his career change, Barnes said: "I was never intending to become a professional musician, but once I realised how important music was to me, I couldn't imagine doing anything else.

"I also wanted something to fall back on. Everyone who's doing music is taking their life in their hands so I studied economics. It's important to have multiple strings to your bow."

Barnes relishes the opportunity to combine his skills. "I have an active mind so I enjoy being able to balance teaching, performing and the administrative side of things. It's a huge job."

Barnes, an international award-winning musician, has participated in four seasons with the World Youth Orchestra during his career as well as being a member of the Adelaide Symphony Orchestra. He performed as principal bassoon with the Sydney and Australian Youth Orchestras for several years while he completed his economics degree.

As a youngster, he studied with John Cran, who was the Sydney Symphony's principal bassoonist for more than 30 years. He later studied with renowned bassoonist and current Dean of the Conservatorium, Kim Walker, when she was based in Geneva. He taught chamber music and bassoon at Indiana University in the United States for four years, before deciding to make Australia home.

"Even if students don't pursue music as a career, the discipline and problem-solving skills that you learn through being a musician are a great asset."

Woodwind Chair Andrew Barnes giving a lesson to Alex Farrugia

" The discipline and problem-solving skills that you learn through being a musician are a great asset…everyone who's doing music is taking their life in their hands, but I couldn't imagine doing anything else."

Andrew Barnes, Chair of Woodwind Unit

Saxophone student Harry White rehearsing for a performance with David Miller

Flute students, (from left to right) Natalie Wood, Sarah Anderson, Jessica Lee
and Jane Duncan, waiting their turn to perform

Bassoon student Charles Roest playing in front of a class led by Mark Walton

Lecturer Mark Walton rehearsing the saxophone orchestra

Sarah Anderson playing in the orchestra

"The virtuosity in teaching is being able to turn a sow's ear into a silk purse. It's not about manufacturing students. They have to really, really want to do it because it's a very humiliating process."

Richard McIntyre, former associate principal bassoon with the SSO for
10 years and member of staff at the Conservatorium for 6 years.

Baritone Saxophone students Alison Crocker and Jo Carey rehearsing

Recorder student Alicia Crossley in a practising session

Music Access Centre

Susanne James

Chair, Music Access Centre

"Learning music is not convenient and it's not ordinary." This is the mantra Access Centre Chair Susanne James chants to parents when they enrol their children for lessons.

Enrolling more than 3000 students per year, producing 30 concerts and employing some 160 casual teachers are major achievements but James relishes every moment. Hand-selected to establish the unit in 1995, James left her position as education manager for the Sydney Symphony Orchestra.

She describes her role as "an honourable, ethical job. We see ourselves as custodians, in terms of ensuring the development of music as a very significant part of our culture. Music is an indicator of a civilised society".

Offering courses to students of all ages, James stresses that tertiary courses at the Con are only one aspect of what the institution offers. "It's never been just a tertiary institution. Our job is to open the doors of the Conservatorium to the community. The NSW Government is very keen that this is a public resource, funded by the taxpayer."

"We offer part-time courses for adults who want to learn to sing or play the piano, for example. Most people find they need some creative outlet [and that] they really need a place to go."

On Saturday mornings the Con comes alive with young students and their parents. "In our junior program a lot of the students go on to the Conservatorium High School, and from the senior program they often go to the degree program," James said.

"Parents whose children do any of the arts are so enthusiastic. It's very time consuming and demanding and it's only with parents' incredible patience, commitment and time-management skills that the music lessons are possible."

6 year old Claudia Mackay being taught by Christine Myers

"Learning music is not convenient and it's not ordinary. Parents need incredible patience, commitment and time management skills if their children are to learn music. We have an honorable, ethical job - we see ourselves as custodians who must ensure the development of music as a significant part of our culture."

Susanne James, **Director of the Music Access Centre**

Melissa Farrow teaching a duet to flute student Nina Pace and harp student Dubravka Ilic

Cassandra Lum learning oral skills with the help of a computer

"Musicians should be able to hear - I don't think that's too outrageous a thing to say. Music is not just isolated from social context, it's important to understand where it sits in a cultural context. Students need a basic literacy and understanding of harmony to be able to hear."

Richard Toop, reader, former Chair of Musicology Unit

Kirsten Barry teaching ensemble studies to Alicia Crossley (recorder),
Jeremy So (harpsichord) and Chris Jessup (oboe)

Young cello student Joshua Grasso during a lesson break

Voice teacher Nadia Piave (centre) with a class

Voice teacher Joy Yates doing warm up exercises with students at the beginning of the lesson

Children having fun in the Music Workshop, during a Dalcroze Eurhythmics Class, which aims to teach music concepts through movement

Ron Philpott on drums (foreground) in a rehearsal

Conservatorium High School

Barbara McCrae

Principal, Conservatorium High School

"The trouble with the kids here is that they treat the school like a family." Barbara McCrae chuckled as she related how a member of staff had said this to her a few years ago.

The Conservatorium High School *is* like a family ~ one that you join for a very long time, without realising it at the time. In 2004, the High School had 187 students. "What makes the school special are the kids ~ they find soul mates, friends who also love music. There is an enormous amount of humour around the school and you really miss it when you're away."

Choral work is an important part of life at the Conservatorium High School. Rehearsing for 90 minutes a week, students learn sophisticated vocal techniques. "The choirs are very strong. We had Lyn Williams in at the beginning of the year. She's the conductor of the Sydney Children's Choir... the kids now study more in-depth technique and they sing great works of art."

"I remember walking into a classroom one day and seeing 'Choir is the best part of the day' written up on the blackboard."

McCrae says the choral repertoire is rotated every six years, ensuring that every student has the opportunity to study great works such as the Faure *Requiem* during their time there.

When asked why the school attracted so many dedicated students, McCrae's answer was simple: "It's a stimulating environment. The point of the school is to allow students to balance academic studies with music studies. We do English and maths up to the very top levels."

Student Jamie Leigh Russell attending class in a keyboard lab

Students enjoying some fresh air during lunch break in the Royal Botanic Gardens outside the school

"I came from a country town when I was 15. At home I used to play sonatas with a doctor who was the son of Mr Verbrugghen, the director of the Conservatorium at the time. When I arrived in Sydney, I remember sitting under a tree in the Botanic Gardens and thinking, how long has all this music been going on without me? I was so happy to be part of it."

Mrs Dulcie Magnus, former Conservatorium High School student, now in her 90s.

The Junior Strings with Kathryn Betts

"We were working on some violin and piano sonatas, and he, the first teacher at the Conservatorium High School, Alfred Steele, said: 'To play this piece well, you have to eat lots of raw meat.' He then did the haka, the New Zealand war dance."

Mrs Dagnar Hunstead, former Conservatorium High School student, now in her 90s.

(from left to right) Kartini Suharto-Martin, Minh-Thi Tran and Loretta Cheung relaxing during school recess

"When I played a gig many years ago a seven-year-old child came up to me and said, ' I never knew the sound of someone dreaming came from the harp.' It made it all worthwhile."

Lyn Williams, conductor of the Sydney Children's Choir and harpist

Lyn Williams conducting the Conservatorium High School Orchestra

Netta Dor playing the bassoon

Natalie Stepanian in the keyboard lab

(From left to right), Kartika Suharto-Martin, Joanna Brooke, Laura Geran, Oliver Boyle and Sharon Wang at a Junior Strings rehearsal

Violin student Aiden Abeni-Davis

(From left to right) William Shreeve, Christopher Ng and James Hocking during recess

View of the Conservatorium from inside the Royal Botanic Gardens. On this side at
ground level is the entrance to the Conservatorium High School

Into the Future

Kim Walker
Dean from 2004

Exploring the creative mind is the passion of musical dynamo Kim Walker. Describing her appointment as "serendipitous," she heard about the position at the Con during a visit to Sydney at the time Sharman Pretty announced her resignation.

The first non-Australian to take the reins since Eugene Goosens in 1948, Walker has a passion for integrating music with the other arts. She joined the faculty of Indiana University as professor of bassoon in 1994 and chaired the woodwind department.

Subsequent appointments broadened her involvement in arts administration. These included Artistic Director of the Summer Music Festival for the Millennium, Associate Dean of Academic Affairs and Dean of the Faculties, Associate Dean of Research on the office of the Vice President and finally Director of Arts and Cultural Outreach in the Office of the President at Indiana University.

Walker's administrative skills are the icing on the cake of what has been a distinguished musical career.

"By 26 I was performing with the London Symphony and the Chamber Orchestra of Europe," she said. "Eventually my solo career took over [she has 23 recordings to her name]. "Building a career as a solo bassoonist required a strategic approach rather than collecting isolated moments of success... this required extensive research of libraries all over Europe for unpublished music, commissioning new works, developing contacts."

Walker took a systematic approach to administration based on experience. "I had bank accounts in five different countries, so I hired someone to be my personal manager and gave them a percentage."

Exuding a positive attitude and limitless enthusiasm, it is no surprise that Walker managed to attract a large amount of funding for Indiana University during her tenure there. "Raising this money was the result of building extensive partnerships, affiliations and collaborations between the art forms... by showcasing the public consequences of creative activity we were able to attract major donors."

She has assisted her students to gain employment all over the world. One of her former students, Andrew Barnes, chairs the Con's Woodwind Unit.

Practical innovations that yield practical results are what this woman is about and her approach augurs well for the Conservatorium's future.